SANTA'S MAGIC CHRISTMAS STORIES

A Unique Christmas Book for Children about Love, Inspiration and Friendship | Gift for Girls and Boys

Christmas Friends and Family

ISBN – 9798754215696

THIS BOOK BELONGS TO

....

....

CONTENTS

Story 1

THE RUNAWAY CHRISTMAS PUDDING

It was a disaster!

Samantha ran through the house, shouting for her brother, Tom. The Christmas pudding was missing! She'd been helping Mummy and Daddy set the table for dinner when she realised that the pudding wasn't in the cupboard anymore.

"What's wrong?" Tom asked, coming out of his room.

"The Christmas pudding is gone!" Samantha told him. "Quick, we need to find it before Grandma and Grandpa come over for dinner later".

"Slow down!"

Samantha was dragging Tom behind her, not wanting to waste any time. It was only the 10th of December, but Grandma and Grandpa had been living abroad for three years, so Mummy had decided that they should have an early Christmas dinner before the actual day.

The kitchen was mayhem. There were huge pots of carrots and potatoes and broccoli and peas everywhere, as well as a massive turkey in the oven. It smelled amazing, but there was no time to stop. She had no idea where the pudding could have gone, but nobody had seen it since the morning.

"Where should we start looking?" Samantha asked Tom. "I've looked everywhere inside the house, but it's like the pudding has completely disappeared".

"A runaway Christmas pudding," Tom laughed. "Let's check outside".

They put on their coats, scarves and gloves and went outside. The entire garden looked magical, as if a huge white blanket had fallen over the grass and the trees.

"Do you know why it's so cold at Christmas?" Tom asked.

"Why?"

"Because it's Decembrrr!"

Samantha laughed at his joke, but she was looking around for the Christmas pudding. The snow was almost perfect, except for under the tree at the end of the garden. There was a gap, as if something had burrowed under the snow. Maybe the pudding had run out of the house and tried to get cosy under the snow?

"Over here," she said, pulling Tom with her.

When they got to the gap, they didn't find the turkey. Instead, they found a hole just big enough for a person to fit through that seemed to lead underground. There was an amazing smell coming from it, almost like someone was cooking roast potatoes.

"What do you think is down there?" Samantha questioned.

"There's only one way to find out!" Tom replied.

He carefully lowered Samantha down through the hole and then jumped down himself. He almost got stuck around the shoulders, but Samantha pulled his leg until he fell down next to her. They were standing inside a tunnel and there were sounds of movement and music at the end.

"What do you think is down there?" Samantha whispered.

"I don't know, but I hope it's not rabbits," Tom responded, remembering how scared he used to be of rabbits.

"I just thought of a joke about rabbits," Samantha said. "What do you call a rabbit with too many blankets in his burrow? A hot cross bunny!"

Tom laughed, leading the way down the tunnel. The sounds got louder as they turned the corner and looked in amazement at what they saw.

There was an entire village under their garden and it was decorated for Christmas! All the houses were small, so Samantha could see inside the windows and Tom was taller than the chimneys. They all had tiny Christmas trees with tinsel and lights and stars at the top, and colourful presents wrapped up underneath. When she looked closely, Samantha could see tables with food and drink laid out.

"This all looks so wonderful, like a Christmas dream!"

"I wonder if the pudding ran away to live here," Tom said.

They followed the sound of music to what looked like a town square and it really did look like a Christmas dream. It had lots of Christmas lights everywhere, which reminded Samantha of when she and Tom would go to see the lights in the city with Mummy and Daddy. But there were crowds of tiny people in bright outfits dancing around something in the middle of the square.

It was their Christmas pudding!

"Can you see it?" She said, nudging Tom.

"Yes," he replied. "Our pudding has been stolen by pixies".

Samantha had never seen pixies before, so she didn't think they could be real. But there were hundreds of pixies right in front of her eyes now, all dancing around the Christmas pudding.

"Who are you?" Asked a voice.

Samantha and Tom turned around to see a pixie in a Christmas jumper standing behind them. He was about as tall as Samantha, so Tom looked like a giant next to him.

"I'm Samantha and this is Tom. We live in the house above the ground".

"So you're the ones who brought us this feast," the pixie beamed. "Everyone! We've got visitors!"

The pixie, who quickly introduced himself as Glimmer, led Samantha and Tom to the middle of the square. Their Christmas pudding had been transformed by magic and was now bigger than them both! There was more than enough to go around.

"How did the pudding get down here?" Tom asked Glimmer.

"Well, we were hunting through the snow for things to add to our Christmas dinner when we noticed your window was open," the pixie explained. "So, I tiptoed through with two of my friends,

Snowdrop and Stardust, and we picked up the pudding while the bigger humans weren't looking".

Those mischievous pixies!

"Well, as magical as the pudding looks now, we really do need it for our early Christmas dinner," Samantha said.

"I see," Glimmer mused. "I'll tell you what, if you can answer a riddle then we'll give you back the pudding and we can be friends".

Samantha nodded. "We accept".

"What has plenty of needles, but doesn't know how to sew?"

"Do you have any ideas?" Samantha whispered to Tom.

He shook his head and turned to Glimmer. "Can we have a hint?"

"No hints!" The pixie declared.

Samantha looked around, wondering if anything would inspire her thoughts. She looked at the house closest to them and saw all the tinsel hanging from the branches of the tree.

That was it!

"A Christmas tree," she answered.

Glimmer laughed. "Very good! I suppose that makes us friends now. And we'll give you back your pudding".

The pixies magicked the pudding back to its regular size and bid farewell to Samantha and Tom, promising that they'd see them again soon. After all, they were friends now.

"Would you like a bit of pudding?" Samantha asked before they left. "If you just take a little bit, I'm sure nobody will notice".

"That's very kind," said Glimmer.

"Christmas is about sharing and making sure everyone has fun," Samantha told him. "I love sharing with my friends, and now we'll all get to have some pudding".

And throughout their dinner, she and Tom kept smiling at each other, knowing that their new friends the pixies just below the ground were having a fine dinner because of them. Christmas Day hadn't even arrived yet, but it had already given them the gift of some magical new friends.

Story 2

THE REINDEER WHO LEARNED TO FLY

Zack was bored.

He never thought that he could be bored with so much to do during the Christmas season, but he was by himself in his bedroom because everybody else was busy preparing things or buying presents or shovelling snow out on the streets. He really wanted to play, but all his friends were busy today.

He decided that he'd go and play in the park down the street. After wrapping up warm, he walked towards the park, noticing that there were already tiny prints in the snow, They looked like hooves, but the park seemed empty.

"Hello?" Zack called. "Is anyone there?"

He heard a rustle behind him and saw a reindeer emerging from the bushes!

"Hello," it said. "My name is Stanley".

"That's an unusual name for a reindeer," Zack replied. "Most of the others have names like Dasher and Prancer and Rudolph".

"Those are the names of the senior reindeer," Stanley told him. "The rest of us mainly work around the North Pole".

"So you know Rudolph?" Zack asked.

"I do. Hey, what do you call Rudolph in a bakery?" Joked Stanley. "Rudolph the Bread-Nosed Reindeer!"

Zack laughed. "Is his nose really that bright?"

"Yes, it lights up all of Santa's workshop when he stops by. He doesn't have as much time to spend with all of us now though, he's always too busy practising for when he leads Santa's sleigh on Christmas Eve. It's always been a dream of mine to pull the sleigh too".

"So why haven't you done it?"

Stanley sighed. "There are only a few places for reindeer to pull the sleigh. Comet broke his leg in training, so they're looking for a reindeer to take his place this year. The only problem is that I can't fly".

"I thought all Santa's reindeer could fly," Zack exclaimed.

"We have to learn," the reindeer went on. "I can't seem to do it though, despite how much I've been practising. Maybe I don't have the strength to do it".

"Of course you do!" Zack insisted. "I had to have my tonsils taken out a few months ago. I was really scared. But then I realised that if I kept on doubting myself, I'd never find the strength to face my fears. I tried my best to be as brave as possible and I discovered that the surgery really wasn't scary at all!"

"That is good advice," Stanley said. "Maybe if I stop doubting myself, I'll get the hang of flying".

"I'll help you to learn," Zack told him. "Let's use the top part of the park because we'll have lots of space there".

They walked through the park together and Zack decided to try out some Christmas jokes that he'd thought of on Stanley.

"What did the Christmas present say at the end of his work meeting? Let's get this wrapped up!"

"What did Santa say when he couldn't find his sack? No-no-no!"

"What do elves learn at school? The elfabet!"

Stanley laughed at each joke and told Zack fantastic stories about the North Pole and Santa's workshop where they made the presents and the endless amounts of snow. Zack hoped that one day he would get to visit, though he knew that Santa and the elves would be busy preparing for Christmas all year round.

They made it to the top of the park and Stanley started to explain how reindeers learn to fly.

"You have to focus on the feeling of flying and will your legs to lift you off the ground and into the air," he said. "It's all about believing that you can fly. Once you believe, you'll have the strength to do it".

He tried to demonstrate, but barely got off the ground. Zack watched, deep in thought. There had to be something more that could inspire Stanley to fly.

"What is your favourite thing about Christmas?" He asked the reindeer.

"There are so many," was the response. "I love the snow and the food and the decorations. In fact, my favourite part of Christmas is when we all gather outside on Christmas Eve after having a huge dinner and watch the sleigh fly off with all the presents".

"Imagine that," Zack said, "but imagine yourself as one of the reindeer pulling the sleigh instead".

Stanley closed his eyes, tapped the ground with his front hoof, took a deep breath, and galloped. He ran a circle around Zack, but then he started to float! He was very shaky, but Zack shouted encouragement to him and Stanley galloped even harder and got even higher.

Soon enough, the reindeer was galloping through the air right above Zack's head!

Stanley whinnied in triumph and then slowly lowered himself back down to the ground. He trotted on the spot, thrusting his antlers into the air.

"I actually flew!" He exclaimed. "I used all my strength to imagine myself pulling the sleigh and it worked. I don't know how to repay you".

"You don't need to repay me," Zack said. "I'm glad I managed to help you. Now you'll be able to return to the North Pole and save Christmas by helping to pull the sleigh".

Stanley hopped on the spot. "Leave an extra carrot out for me!"

Zack promised that he would and then Stanley trotted away to go back home and ask Santa if he could be Comet's replacement.

On Christmas Eve, Zack pretended to sleep until he was sure Mummy and Daddy had gone to bed. Then, he snuck over to his bedroom window and looked up at the moon. He could see a shape moving in front of it and knew that it was Santa's sleigh. There was a faint red light at the front that must be Rudolph.

Towards the back, he could see one reindeer galloping through the air faster than any of the others. He waved to Stanley, though the reindeer was much too high up to see him, and wanted to jump for joy that his friend had found the strength to face his fears and pull the sleigh. Christmas was saved!

Story 3

ICE SKATING WITH FAIRIES

Clara had always wanted to be a fairy.

She spent so much time learning how to dance and be graceful, but she wanted to really glide and soar and float. The ice rink had seemed like a great idea because she'd be able to glide smoothly along as if she was walking on air. Her two best friends, Emily and Tia, wanted to come too because the whole rink was decorated beautifully for Christmas.

However, when they were queueing up to get their skates, Clara was struck by nerves. The rink was so big and filled with people. She'd never been ice skating before. What if she slipped and then couldn't get back up?

"Are you nervous?" She asked Emily.

"Maybe a bit," Emily replied. "I went ice skating last Christmas as well and there were so many other people about. They were skating really fast and I couldn't keep up. Right before we left, I slipped on the ice".

"Did you hurt yourself?" Tia asked.

"I wasn't injured, but it did scare me. Maybe you should only ice skate if you're good at it".

"We're being such cowards," Clara whispered, grabbing her skates from the counter and walking away with her friends.

"Don't say that".

The three girls looked up, wondering who had spoken. They couldn't see anyone, but then a glimpse of fantastic green caught their eye. There was a girl standing right next to them in a beautiful green dress and matching ice skates. No, not a girl, a fairy! Her wings were glimmering and reminded the friends of Christmas snow.

"Who are you?" Clara gasped.

"My name is Twinkle," replied the fairy, fluttering her wings. "I'm the Ice Rink Fairy and I'm here to help you".

"Ice Rink Fairy?" Emily asked.

"Yes. You see, every Christmas attraction has a fairy watching over it. I watch over the ice rink with my friend, Moonlight, who is the Ice Skating Fairy. She makes sure that everybody has ice skates when they get onto the rink, then I protect them".

"Where is Moonlight?" Clara questioned, still shocked that she was talking to a fairy.

"She's gone to the hot dog stand, but she'll be back soon," Twinkle laughed. "One thing to know about fairies is that we do love hot dogs!"

It was only a moment later when Moonlight appeared. She was wearing a blue dress with matching skates. Twinkle introduced her to the girls, already knowing all their names.

"So, what's the problem here?" Moonlight asked.

"We're worried about skating," Tia answered. "None of us are very good. We're scared of falling".

"Fear is the biggest enemy of happiness," Twinkle told them, "because being too scared to do something means missing out on amazing experiences! All you need to do is find your courage and then you'll make great Christmas memories skating".

Moonlight flew out onto the rink and Twinkle led the girls to the edge, encouraging them onto the ice.

Clara stepped out onto the ice first, then Emily, then Tia. All three of them were wobbling nervously on their skates, looking out at the massive rink before them.

Twinkle beckoned to them. "Come on! I'll guide you. We just have to take it one step at a time".

Clara started to skate out slowly, keeping her arms out to balance herself. She saw Moonlight skating around the rink in a circle and realised that the other fairy was casting a spell to keep the other skaters further away from the three friends. Feeling confident, she tried to go faster and almost fell.

"I've got you!" Twinkle appeared behind her and immediately steadied her. "Now, you can do this".

Emily was a bit further ahead and though she wobbled at times, she was skating! Tia and Clara held hands and slowly glided forwards on their own skates. With Twinkle behind them shouting encouragement and Moonlight practically flying around the rink, the three girls had found the courage to skate. They were actually enjoying it and they weren't scared at all!

"I feel like a fairy," Clara laughed.

"But you don't need wings," Twinkle reminded her. "You've got courage and that's all you need when you really put your mind to something".

Emily attempted to do a twirl. Moonlight threw a small handful of fairy dust in her direction to keep her balanced on the ice. Tia skated up to her and the two girls spun round together, laughing and gliding about as if they were in a fairytale.

They skated on the rink for hours and only stopped when they grew tired. Twinkle and Moonlight glided off the ice with them and followed the three friends on their way to get hot chocolate. Clara asked if the fairies wanted drinks, but Moonlight told her that they could use a spell. With wide eyes, the girls watched the fairy perform yet another wonderful spell and conjure up two hot chocolates.

"I would love to learn magic," Clara sighed.

"There is magic in you too," Twinkle replied. "You found the courage to skate, even though you were afraid. Overcoming your fears is the most magical thing in the world because if you can do that, you can do anything".

"Have you two ever been to the North Pole?" Tia asked.

Moonlight shook her head. "The one thing that fairies hate most of all is the cold! But we have met Santa before".

Three gasps. "Really?"

"Yes," Twinkle smiled. "Sometimes, the reindeer need to eat carrots while they're flying Santa over the sea to deliver gifts to children in other countries, so the fairies fly food up to them. If they got too hungry, they'd have to stop flying, and then thousands of children wouldn't receive their gifts".

"We're lucky to have you then," Clara said.

And they were. The three friends had realised that, though magic was amazing, the true magic was the inspiration to succeed. That inspiration could only come from courage, and they were adamant that they'd never forget the lesson that the fairies had taught them about courage.

Story 4

THE GIFT OF GIVING

Jennifer had just had the greatest idea!

Her older sister, Penny, was feeling sad because she'd broken her arm and Jennifer desperately wanted to cheer her up. She only had a little bit of pocket money left, but she was going to use it to buy materials and make Penny a wonderful Christmas gift.

She asked Daddy if he would take her shopping on the weekend, but when he asked what she wanted to buy, she told him it was a secret. He smiled and agreed to take her on Saturday.

They went into the craft store and Daddy went to go and look at some paints while Jennifer gathered her own supplies. She bought some fabric, a sewing needle, some colourful threads and a box of beads. Luckily, she had just enough pocket money to pay for it all.

Back at home, she sat in her bedroom and got to work on the gift. She was going to try and stitch together an angel for Penny to put at the top of the Christmas tree. Their family used to have an angel, but unfortunately it got lost when they were moving to their new house. This was their first Christmas in the new house and Jennifer wanted to make it special.

She had received a book about sewing from her grandmother last Christmas, but she hadn't tried any of the designs yet. The angel was quite simple, but there were lots of steps to follow. Mummy had trusted her with the scissors because she needed to cut the fabric up and Jennifer felt very grown up.

Her favourite teddy bear, Snuggles, was sat next to her on the floor. She decided to tell him a Christmas joke.

"Snuggles," she said, "what did the angel say to the Christmas tree? You light up my world!"

Snuggles didn't talk, but Jennifer imagined that he was laughing at her joke.

She stitched together the body first, giving the angel a pink and white dress. The halo and wings would be shimmery gold, with a small strip of gold fabric on the bottom of the dress to match. The angel's arms and legs were a bit floppy, but Jennifer thought that Penny wouldn't mind.

She stitched the face delicately and used two beads for the eyes. It could have been her imagination, but she thought she saw the angel wink at her. The angel's hair was made of yellow silk and Jennifer sewed a few beads into it in a wonky line beneath the halo.

She held up the angel and smiled at her work. Then, she had a terrible thought.

"Oh no!" She exclaimed to Snuggles. "I don't have anything to wrap the gift in".

Jennifer turned to look about the room and then blinked in shock. Behind her, there was a gift box wrapped up in green paper with a huge red ribbon bow on top! It looked like the perfect box for a Christmas present, though she had no idea where it had come from.

She glanced around the room, but nobody was there. When she moved closer to the box, she saw that there was a glitter around it. It looked magical! The red and green made her think of Santa's elves. Daddy had told her that the elves often left the North Pole to keep an eye on all the children for Santa, so they must have delivered a box for her special gift for Penny!

Carefully, Jennifer picked up the angel and placed her inside the box. The lid hopped onto the box all by itself and the bow tightened up neatly. The glitter was still sparkling, so Jennifer knew it was magic. She just hoped that Penny would like her gift.

Downstairs, Penny was sat on the sofa near the Christmas tree. Her arm was in a sling and Jennifer knew that it must suck because it would be harder for her sister to play in the snow and wrap presents and hang up decorations. Hopefully her gift would make Penny smile.

She walked into the room with the box behind her back.

Penny looked up. "What have you got there?"

"It's a present for you," Jennifer told her.

"Really?" Penny's eyes lit up as she took the box from her younger sister. "This paper is beautiful".

Jennifer smiled, thankful for the magical assistance. The angel was perfectly safe inside the box. Penny undid the ribbon carefully with her good hand and then eased the lid off.

"An angel," she said.

"I made it," Jennifer replied. "I know I'm not very good at sewing, but I wanted to make a special Christmas gift for you. I spent the last of my pocket money on the materials because I wanted to cheer you up. You're sad about your arm".

Penny said nothing for a moment. But then, she threw her good arm around Jennifer and squeezed her tightly. Jennifer hugged her back.

"It's the best gift I've ever had," Penny told her. "I'm so lucky to have such a compassionate little sister".

"Grandpa always says that Christmas is the time of year to be as kind as you possibly can," Jennifer said.

"But you spent all the pocket money you had left to make a present for me. It's definitely the most perfect gift you can give".

Jennifer beamed and watched her sister reach up to carefully place the angel on top of the tree. She fit just right and looked down at them both. Her golden wings and halo were practically glowing. Penny put her good arm around Jennifer.

"I think the angel will bring us lots of Christmas luck," she said.

Jennifer peered up to the top of the tree again and noticed that the angel had some of the sparkle from the gift box on her. The floppy left arm lifted in a tiny wave before it dropped back to the angel's side.

Penny had received a gift, but so had Jennifer: the gift of giving. And that compassionate gift was priceless.

Story 5

DECORATING THE STREET

"Do you know what I love most about Christmas?"

Ben turned to look at his brother, Adam. "What?"

"The decorations!" Adam answered. Don't you think that those are the real magic of Christmas?"

"I do enjoy putting up the tree," Ben said. "It would be nice to have more decorations, though. The street always looks so empty, no colours or lights".

"I wish there was something that we could do about that," Adam sighed. "If I could have one Christmas wish, it would be for more decorations".

They went to sleep that night, fully unaware that someone had been listening. It was one of Santa's elves who went by the name of Ivy. She'd been visiting the street to collect Christmas wishes for Santa. Lots of children had wishes for special gifts, or for family members and friends to come and visit. She collected the wishes and brought them back to the North Pole for Santa to grant.

Adam's Christmas wish for more decorations was collected up with the others and Ivy took them straight to Santa.

"This is an interesting wish," he said. "There is true generosity in it, the desire to extend Christmas festivities to those around you. We will grant this one before Christmas Day".

And, sure enough, when Adam and Ben woke up the next day, there was a huge box in their bedroom. Ben got out of bed first and picked up the note on top.

Ho, ho, ho! Your wish has been granted. Decorate the street and make sure that you go to bed early on Christmas Eve.

— Santa

"Santa heard our wish!" He exclaimed.

Adam tumbled out of bed and ran over. He read the note too and clapped his hands with glee. The two brothers raced to get washed and dressed, eager to head outside and start decorating the street with Santa's magical decorations. When they looked out of the window, the street, the pavements and all the houses were plain white, covered with a perfect sheet of snow.

"Don't those look like hoof prints?" Adam observed, pointing just outside their house.

Ben looked down. "I think they are! One of Santa's reindeer must have delivered the decorations to us".

The box of decorations was heavy, but between the two of them, Adam and Ben managed to heft it outside. They looked about, wondering where to start.

"Let's put some up on this tree," Adam suggested. "We can turn it into a Christmas tree".

"Do you want to hear my favourite joke about Christmas trees?" Ben asked.

"Of course".

"Why did the Christmas tree need to see a doctor?"

"I don't know. Why did it need to see a doctor?"

"Because it was looking very green!"

Adam laughed. "I've just thought of a joke too. Why was the Christmas tree's friend upset with him? Because he was being very prickly!"

The two boys kept swapping jokes as they decorated the tree. Soon enough, it was covered in festive lights and baubles, yet the box was still full.

"It must have a spell on it," Ben said, "so that we never run out of decorations".

One of their neighbours, an elderly man called Mr Stiles, came out of his house. "What are you boys doing?"

"We thought it would be nice to decorate the street for Christmas this year, Mr Stiles," Adam answered.

Mr Stiles squinted at them. The brothers both froze, wondering if he was going to shout at them. But then, a smile split his face and he laughed.

"That sounds like a wonderful idea," he told them. "Why don't you come and put some decorations up in my garden?"

Adam and Ben grinned at each other. They brought over their magical box of decorations and put them all over Mr Stiles' garden. In no time at all, it looked like a Christmas wonderland!

The bright lights and the colourful baubles and tinsel were soon catching the attention of all the other neighbours. They had never realised before how bare the street looked at Christmas, a time when it was supposed to be as fun and festive and vibrant as possible. Everyone wanted Ben and Adam to decorate their gardens.

"You're both very generous boys," said their next-door neighbour, an elderly lady called Mrs Small. "And what better time to show generosity and help those around you than at Christmas?"

"We're happy to help!" Ben told her.

She peered into their box of decorations. "I'm glad that you've got enough decorations for the entire street in one box as well. It's almost as if they're magical".

Both brothers looked at her and she winked with a knowing smile on her face. Santa's magic had spread across the entire street! Nobody questioned why the Christmas lights worked outside without needing to be plugged in. They just enjoyed the colours and how beautiful they looked.

Best of all, the neighbours rewarded Ben and Adam's generous act with lots of cookies and mugs of hot chocolate! Their wish had been to decorate the street for Christmas, but they hadn't thought about just how happy it would make everyone. They knew that Christmas was a time to decorate and celebrate, but they had learned even more that it was also a time to spread joy to others and show generosity.

After all, their elderly neighbours weren't able to put up decorations themselves, so Adam and Ben were very generous to help them. They had turned the street into the most festive place it could be, and they knew that Santa would be proud of them.

They walked home together, passing endless displays of decorations. Every house was alive with colour and all the people were beaming.

"Where did you boys get to?" Mummy asked when they got inside the house.

"We were decorating the street," Ben told her. "Mrs Small told us that it was a very generous thing to do".

She peered out of the window. "Wow! Where did you get all those decorations?"

Adam and Ben smiled at each other. That was between the two of them and Santa.

Story 6

A GARDEN OF SNOWMEN

Thomas' favourite part of the Christmas season was when the snow started to fall.

As soon as he got out of bed every morning, he opened the curtains and looked outside for snow. He was always disappointed until the morning when he'd open the curtains and see nothing but white. When that morning finally came, he was always elated, and this year was no different.

He went running down the hallway in his pyjamas, his feet already feeling cold because the house got very chilly when it was winter.

"Mummy! Daddy! Wake up!"

Thomas practically flew into their room and jumped on the bed. He did this every year because he wanted them to get up and look at the snow too. It was just a shame that Daddy always had to go to work, so he wouldn't be able to play in the snow with

Thomas. Mummy did instead, but she couldn't this year because she was going to have a baby, so she didn't want to get cold.

"Let me guess, it's snowing?" Daddy laughed and tossed Thomas up into the air and caught him.

Thomas laughed delightedly. "Yes! I can't wait to play in it".

"Well," Daddy said. "I know that I never get the chance to play in the snow with you on the first day, so I've decided to take the day off work".

"Really?"

"Really". The man smiled. "I'll just make a quick phone call, then we can go and play".

"Make sure you wrap up warm, Thomas," Mummy told him.

He couldn't run back to his room quick enough! Frantically, Thomas grabbed his hat, his scarf, his gloves, a warm Christmas jumper, and his coat. He dressed himself and then went downstairs to find Daddy already waiting for him by the door.

"How about we make a snowman before breakfast," he said.

Thomas nodded. "That sounds wonderful! Maybe we can make a really big snowman".

They decided to build the snowman right in the middle of the garden so that they'd have lots of snow to work with. Daddy said that he'd roll the bottom half into a massive snowball. Thomas went around collecting handfuls of snow to add to it.

"Do you know what else a snowman needs?" Daddy asked.

"Arms, eyes, a mouth and some buttons," Thomas answered. "So we can use sticks and rocks".

"But what about the most important bit?"

"Most important?"

"The nose!"

Thomas gasped, wondering how he'd forgotten the nose. "Of course! We need a carrot".

"Go and grab one from the fridge," Daddy told him. "The rest are being saved for the reindeer on Christmas Eve".

Thomas ran inside and grabbed a carrot from the fridge. He was just about tall enough to reach and he imagined how tall he'd be next Christmas. Back outside, he found his father making a start on the top half of the snowman's body.

"We'll make the head next and you can add the carrot," he told Thomas." Hey, what do snow rabbits eat? Frosty carrots!"

Thomas laughed at the joke. "I have a joke too. Why did the snowman go to see a doctor? Because he had frostbite!"

The two of them kept coming up with Christmas jokes as they built the snowman. Thomas added three black rocks to be the buttons on the body and two sticks in the sides for arms. Then, they made the head and Daddy lifted him up to help him put the eyes, mouth and nose on. Thomas especially loved sticking the carrot into the snowman's face and seeing him come together properly.

"This is definitely the best snowman I've ever seen," the young boy declared.

"It's the best I've ever seen too," Daddy agreed. "But he needs a scarf".

He took off his own scarf and wrapped it around the snowman's neck. It looked perfect! Thomas loved everything about Christmas, but snow was definitely his favourite. This snowman was better than any he'd built by himself in the past.

"What do you want to call him?"

Thomas thought for a moment. "What about Icy? He could be Frosty the Snowman's brother!"

"That's a good name," Daddy said. Then, he paused. "Thomas, I hope you know how much I love you".

Thomas looked up at his father. "Of course I do, it's Christmas!"

"But it's important to show and recognise love all year round. I'm sorry that I haven't been able to spend the first day of snow playing outside with you for a while. From now on, we're going to build lots of snowmen".

Thomas hugged his father warmly. He knew how important love was, but he thought that it was even more special to share love at Christmas. It was the end of one year and the beginning of a new one. He wanted to end the year with love and start the next year with even more love.

When the hug ended, they looked around and were surprised to find the garden filled with snowmen. Their snowman was in the middle of an entire snowman society! The two of them stood in the middle too, looking at all the other snowmen in wonder.

"It's a magical Christmas miracle!" Thomas exclaimed.

Daddy laughed. "It really is".

All the snowmen had perfect smiles made out of lumps of coal. They were all looking at the snowman in the middle. The garden was a wonderland and every bit of snow that formed the snowmen was inspired by the love and Christmas spirit of Thomas and his father.

Story 7

AN EVENING OF CAROLS

"There are so many people out there!"

Amanda peered around the stage curtain, taking in the massive crowd in shock. There were so many people who had come to listen to the Christmas carols!

She was going to be singing with her two best friends, Rebecca and Sara. They'd been practising all year round for this performance, determined not to make any mistakes or forget any of the words. Amanda imagined that, by now, her blood was probably red and green because she'd absorbed so much Christmas spirit.

Rebecca squashed up next to her. "Can you see my parents?"

"Get back, you two!" Sara hissed. "Miss Lucy said that we have to stay behind the curtain out of sight until it's our turn to sing".

Miss Lucy was their singing teacher. She'd been sure to tell them all about how to act when backstage. The three girls loved Miss Lucy because she always made the singing lessons so festive, even when it wasn't Christmas. Amanda, Sara and Rebecca had spent the year counting down the days until the Christmas carols performance.

But now, the nerves were starting to seep in. The girls had beautiful singing voices, but the thought of singing in front of so many people was beginning to destroy their confidence.

"That girl in the red dress is so pretty," Amanda said, pointing to the girl who was singing on the stage.

"And her voice is amazing," Sara added. "I know that I can't sing as good as that".

Rebecca was looking a little green in the face. "What if we make fools of ourselves? I don't think I want to sing".

There was a sound behind them and then Miss Lucy appeared, seemingly out of thin air. She was wearing a green sparkly dress that made her look like a fabulous Christmas tree.

"What's wrong?" She asked. "Why don't you want to sing?"

"We're too nervous," Amanda told her.

"But you've always sung so well in your lessons!"

"It's the stage," Rebecca sighed. "I don't think I can do it".

"But don't you think people want to hear you sing? You all have such wonderful voices and everyone has come together here just to hear you sing Christmas songs!"

The three girls still looked unconvinced, the nerves having completely taken over them now.

"I know what you need," she said, smiling. "You need to believe in a little Christmas spirit!"

And then, like festive magic, two shimmering wings appeared on Miss Lucy's back! The girls gasped and stared, barely able to believe their eyes. Their singing teacher was a fairy?

"It's not every day you get to see a fairy, is it?" Miss Lucy asked.

"I can't believe it!" Amanda exclaimed. "But☐ if you're a fairy, why did you disguise yourself as a singing teacher?"

"Every fairy has their own purpose," Miss Lucy explained. "I am the Christmas Spirit Fairy, so it is my job to spread as much inspiration and joy as possible! I wanted to teach you all to sing carols because people love them at Christmas. But now I realise that what you three really need is self-confidence".

"Do you have a spell for that?" Sara questioned.

"No, but I do have some magic words for you to remember. Believe in yourselves. If you don't, you'll never have the confidence to do what you love, and I know you all love singing and

Christmas. It's important to share festive joy, so get out onto the stage and embrace the true spirit of Christmas!"

Amanda took a deep breath and stepped out onto the stage. Sara followed her, then Rebecca. The three of them were holding their carol sheets, motivated by Miss Lucy's important advice. When they got to the middle of the stage, the three girls stood together, preparing to sing.

They heard the music start and when they looked up, they could see Miss Lucy playing the piano. She truly had the most beautiful wings! Next to her, an elf was playing the tambourine. A second elf was further back, playing the bells.

The girls started to sing 'Jingle Bells'. They kept repeating Miss Lucy's words about self-confidence and having faith in yourself in their heads. Soon, all their nerves were completely gone and they could do nothing but sing. Their voices sounded as beautiful as ever, and they didn't even need to look at the carol sheets for the words.

The song finished and everyone applauded. Next, they sang, 'Rudolph, the Red-Nosed Reindeer'. The elf who was playing the bells danced around while ringing them, filling the entire room with a jingling sound. Their third song was 'Winter Wonderland', then 'Santa Claus Is Comin' To Town', and finally 'We Wish You A Merry Christmas'.

Once the performance was over and the girls were off the stage, Miss Lucy flew over to them. She was grinning from ear to ear.

"So, how did you feel?" She asked.

"It was amazing!" Amanda said. "Thank you for reminding me how important it is to believe in yourself, it made me feel so much more self-confident".

"The first step is to believe," Miss Lucy replied, "and after that, you can do anything!"

"We couldn't have done it without you," Rebecca told her.

"Just promise me one thing now. Believe in yourselves all year round because the spirit of Christmas is more than carols, bells and celebrating. It's about having the confidence to show everyone just how much you love Christmas! And being self-confident is the best feeling in the world. Christmas is a time for nothing but good feelings, as you all already know".

The girls nodded and then noticed their parents approaching to congratulate them.

"My work here is done," Miss Lucy said. "Now, I must fly to the North Pole and spread more Christmas spirit there too. The elves need to be motivated, after all!"

"Will you tell Santa we said Merry Christmas?" Sara asked.

Miss Lucy laughed. "Of course. He loves it when children wish him a Merry Christmas".

The three friends watched her fly away, knowing that they'd never forget what they'd learned during their evening of carols. Santa knew too, and he was happy for them.

IT'S THE THOUGHT THAT COUNTS

Dylan loved spending days in December at Grandma's house.

She always had her entire house decorated in the most festive way, with decorations shaped like Santa's reindeer and sleigh in the garden. She had decorations shaped like elves climbing up the walls of the house and a huge Santa decoration on the roof that lit up. He had his massive sack full of presents over his shoulder, ready to slide down the chimney and eat all the mince pies left out below.

When Dylan asked how the Santa decoration got up on the roof, Grandma smiled and told him that it was because of Christmas magic. Then he wondered if Santa was shocked when he landed his sleigh on the roof on Christmas Eve and saw a decoration that looked just like him staring back.

Inside the house, Grandma had the tallest Christmas tree that Dylan had ever seen. It had tinsel and lights and baubles and a star at the top. His favourite part of Christmas Day was when they went over to Grandma's house and she'd have all the presents from Santa under the tree.

Today, he was sat on the floor wrapping a present for Mummy that Grandma had helped him to buy. She was sat in her armchair watching.

"Grandma," Dylan spoke up, "can I tell you a joke?"

"Of course," Grandma replied.

"What is red and green and faster than the speed of light?"

"I don't know".

"An elf who is late to Santa's workshop on Christmas Eve!"

Grandma laughed. "You know, I bet that the elf who has to deliver all the children's Christmas letters from around the world to Santa runs even faster".

"Have you written a Christmas wish letter to Santa?" Dylan asked her.

"No, I haven't written one since I was your age," Grandma answered. "I asked Santa for a doll with dark hair and blue eyes. I was very good, so he brought me the doll and left it in a box under the tree. She was wearing a purple dress. Unfortunately, I took her out with me one day and she got lost".

"What was her name?"

"Penelope".

"That's a nice name," Dylan said. "I wrote a wish list for Santa this year, but I can't tell you what was on it because that's a secret between me and Santa".

Grandma smiled knowingly. "Yes, it is. You never even let your grandfather read the letter, did you?"

Dylan shook his head. "I didn't. But he always tried to guess what was on it. Sometimes he was right! He used to say that it was important to be grateful for every gift you receive, even if you didn't ask for that gift, because Christmas is a time to be thankful".

"That's right," Grandma agreed. "Would you like me to tell you a story about him?"

"Yes!"

Dylan scooted along the floor towards Grandma's chair and sat by her feet. He looked up at her, waiting for her to start telling the story.

"When I first met your grandfather," Grandma began, "he had only ever received one Christmas gift because his family didn't have much money and he had never sent Santa a letter. The gift was a watch".

"Did Grandpa like the gift?" Dylan asked.

"Yes, he did. He used to wear it all the time, even after it stopped working. You remember it, don't you?"

Dylan nodded.

"Well, it was very special to your grandfather. He was so grateful for it because it was his only Christmas present. That's why he always talked about gratitude being so important. One year, I asked him if he wanted a new watch for Christmas, but he said no. The watch was too precious to him and he'd never want to wear a different one, even if it was more expensive".

"Everybody says that money isn't what makes a gift special," Dylan agreed, "because Santa wants to give every child toys and make them happy. Most of all, he wants them to be happy because Christmas is such a great time of year. Being happy with toys is just a bonus".

"It's the thought that counts," Grandma said.

She stood up from her armchair and walked over to the drawers across the room. The top drawer had a small box inside and Grandma took it out and opened it. Dylan recognised the watch inside as the special watch that Grandpa always used to wear.

"You'll get lots of presents from Santa," Grandma told him, "but I wanted to give you a special gift from me too. You know how important it is to show gratitude, so I want you to have your grandfather's watch".

Dylan took the watch and then threw his arms around her. "I promise that I'm grateful for this gift and I will show gratitude on Christmas Day and all year round".

In the North Pole, Santa was listening. Though he sent his elves out into the world some time before Christmas, he was also aware of everything that was going on. He knew that Dylan had been very good that year, so he was going to gift him the fire truck that he had written on his Christmas list.

Though she hadn't sent a letter to the North Pole, he wanted to get Dylan's grandmother a special gift too. Of course, the watch that she had gifted Dylan and the lesson about gratitude were the most important, but he knew that she also deserved a magical gift.

"Sparkle," he said, summoning one of the elves.

"Yes, Santa?" Sparkle popped his head around the door.

"I need you to prepare one extra special Christmas gift".

On Christmas Day, Dylan and his parents visited Grandma. He noticed that there was one gift left under the tree. It was wrapped in the most magical silver paper, with a gift tag that simply read:

Ho, ho, ho! Merry Christmas!

    — Santa

"Grandma, it's for you!" He exclaimed.

Grandma took the present from him. "So it is".

She unwrapped the paper carefully and then opened the box. Inside, there was a little doll with dark hair and blue eyes. She was wearing a purple dress, just like the doll that Grandma had lost when she was a child.

Santa watched from the North Pole and smiled.

Story 9

THE ELVES AND THE REINDEER

Amelia adored the markets at Christmas.

So many stalls, all selling amazing things. There were smells of gingerbread, sugar, hot chocolate and cinnamon. People were bustling about everywhere, some of them buying their last presents on Christmas Eve, others mingling with friends and enjoying the atmosphere.

Amelia went every year with her parents. They got hot drinks and cookies and inspected all the stalls. She was always vibrating with excitement because she knew that when she went to sleep that night, she'd be waking up to presents the next day. Santa was always so generous because he appreciated her good behaviour.

She was looking at a stall selling hot chocolate when she lost sight of her parents. Looking about, Amelia knew that they couldn't have gone far. She began walking through the market, peering behind some of the stalls. Then, a rustle of movement in the bushes just outside the marketplace caught her eye.

"Mummy? Daddy?" She called, walking towards the rustling.

"Santa!" That exclamation was all she heard before an elf popped his head out of the bushes.

Amelia gasped. A real elf! And he was looking for Santa. When the elf saw that she wasn't Santa, he hurried to hide himself again.

"Wait!" Cried Amelia, rushing towards him.

When she ran through the bushes, she found two more elves and two reindeer. The reindeer were wearing harnesses that were attached to a cart carrying some presents. Both the cart and the reindeer were stuck in the snow, with the other two elves trying to dig them out.

"That's not Santa, Glow!" Scolded the only female elf. "You've brought us a human!"

"I won't hurt you," Amelia said. "I can see you're having some trouble. Can you tell me your names?"

"I'm Star," said the female elf. "This is Candy. And the one who got your attention is Glow".

The reindeer turned towards Amelia. The first introduced himself as Dasher and the other was Prancer. Two of Santa's favourite reindeer!

"But why aren't you with Santa now?" She asked.

Candy sighed and slumped down on a log with Star and Glow. "We were riding on the sleigh, but then some presents fell off. We got the cart and came with Dasher and Prancer to find them, but then some snow fell off a tree and they got stuck. Now we've lost the sleigh!"

"Oh, you poor things!"

Amelia was saddened by the elf's tale. If they couldn't get back to Santa's sleigh with the reindeer and the presents then Christmas would be ruined for lots of children! She sat down on the log next to the elves, wondering what to do.

"There's no way that we can get Dasher and Prancer out by ourselves," Candy sighed. "If we can't find the sleigh then Christmas will be ruined".

Amelia thought quietly for a moment and then leaped up off the log. "I know! I'll help you push the cart and reindeer free. I'm a human, so I'm a bit stronger than you".

"You'd really help us?" Star said.

"Christmas hope is very important," Candy told her. "It's one of the things that inspires us most in the North Pole! The workshops are all powered by the hope of children waiting for Christmas Day. The sleigh is pulled by the reindeer, but it is also powered by all our hopes for the perfect Christmas".

The four of them gathered behind the cart, preparing to try and push it free from the snow.

"Okay, we'll get you out of the snow," Amelia told the reindeer. "All we've got to do is think about the spirit of Christmas hope and we can do it! We'll push together on three. One, two, three!"

Amelia, Candy, Star and Glow all pushed, but the reindeer and their cart of presents didn't seem to budge. Amelia squeezed her eyes closed and pushed with all her might, thinking about how happy the children would be to receive their presents on Christmas morning. If she couldn't rescue the presents and help the elves and reindeer to get back to the sleigh, all those hopeful children would wake up to no presents!

Suddenly, the reindeer started to move forwards, the cart of presents sliding behind them. Amelia kept pushing, as did the elves, and finally, the reindeer and the presents were almost free of the snow. It took a few more pushes before they were completely free.

The four of them collapsed to the ground, panting. Glow took off his hat and used it as a fan.

"What do you call an elf who gets tired out easily?" Amelia joked.

"I don't know," said Glow.

"Un-elf-thy!"

Glow laughed and shook his head. "Well, I don't feel very unhealthy after all that work!"

"Now we just need to find Santa's sleigh again," Star said. She looked around. "It must be close by, Santa wouldn't go on without us".

"I'll help you," Amelia told them. "I never thought I would get to see an elf, let alone three! I want to help you and the reindeer get back to the sleigh so that all the presents can be delivered".

"Then, hop on!" Dasher said, stomping his hooves on the snowy ground.

Amelia climbed onto the cart with Star, Candy and Glow and they were off. How wonderful it felt to ride on the back of a cart pulled by two of Santa's reindeer, accompanied by three elves! They flew through the snow, all of them calling for Santa. Then, they heard a voice calling back:

"Ho, ho, ho! This way!"

Dasher and Prancer followed the voice and the cart entered a clearing. Right in the middle was Santa's sleigh, full to the brim with presents! There were seven other reindeer, all led by Rudolph, and Santa himself!

"You found the presents!" He laughed.

"We did!" Candy said. "And we made a friend. This is Amelia. She helped us get the cart out of the snow".

Santa turned to the little girl. "Well, Amelia, you've been a very helpful and courageous girl! I'll be sure to leave you an extra special gift tonight".

"Thank you, Santa!" Amelia exclaimed.

The elves had carried the presents back into the sleigh and Dasher and Prancer had joined the other reindeer. Santa cast a little spell over his shoulder before he jumped back into the sleigh, and Amelia's parents came running through the trees.

She hugged them and then all three of them watched in wonder as the sleigh flew up into the air, carrying Santa away with a joyful cry of, "Merry Christmas, everyone!"

Story 10

CELEBRATING CHRISTMAS DAY

"Wake up, wake up, wake up!"

John opened his eyes and felt his bed shaking. When he sat up, he saw his younger sister, Sally, and his younger brother, Joe, jumping up and down at the end.

"It's Christmas Day!" Sally exclaimed, her eyes shining.

"Come on, John," Joe said. "Mummy and Daddy are downstairs making breakfast, but we need to see if Santa and his reindeer came last night!"

"Okay," laughed John, "I'm coming".

He got out of bed and ran after his siblings. They practically flew downstairs together, far too eager to see if Santa had eaten the cookies and had the milk they'd left out. They also left some carrots for the reindeer because they'd need lots of energy to fly Santa's sleigh all across the world in a single night.

When they ran into the living room, the three children clapped their hands with glee and hugged each other.

"Santa ate the cookies and drank the milk!" Sally squealed. "And he took the carrots up the chimney to feed Rudolph and his friends".

"Look at all the presents he left," John added. "The wrapping paper looks magical".

"That's because the elves collect snow in the North Pole to make it," Joe said.

"Really?" Sally asked.

"Yes. They collect lots of snow and all the helper reindeer fly it back to the workshop. Then, the elves put it into a machine that's powered by magic and it makes the paper. When the gifts are all wrapped up, they can't be damaged if they bounce around in the sleigh when Santa is delivering them".

"Wow!"

Mummy walked into the room and hugged each of the children. "Merry Christmas! How about some breakfast before presents?"

The children were eager to open their presents, but they knew it was important to spend time together too, so they went into the kitchen for breakfast. Daddy wished them a "Merry Christmas" too and then put the food on the table. He always made a special

Christmas breakfast with pancakes shaped like reindeer. There was icing sugar sprinkled like snow and the children loved to flick some at each other, pretending to have a snowball fight.

"The quicker you eat, the quicker you can open presents," Mummy reminded them.

The children hurried to eat, trying not to make a mess. Then, once they'd cleared away their plates, they were allowed to head back to the tree. And they'd tried really hard to always be good that year, so Santa had delivered the gifts on their wish letters.

They opened the presents. Sally received the doll's house she asked for, John received a model train set and Joe received the toy cars he had asked for. All three of them were overjoyed, and they were inspired to be even better behaved next year. After all, Christmas was a time to celebrate the whole year and everything it had brought.

Mummy made them get out of their pyjamas for Christmas lunch. Daddy was cooking the turkey while she cooked the potatoes and vegetables. They'd had a great breakfast, but the children were even more excited for lunch. The Christmas turkey and then the pudding afterwards were some of the best bits of the holiday.

"Do you think elves wear pyjamas?" Joe asked John.

"Of course they do," John replied. "But their pyjamas are green and red as well".

"Hey, what do you call an elf who won't share the Christmas pudding? Elfish!"

John laughed at the joke. "What instruments do elves play in the Christmas music show? Jingle bells!"

They went downstairs again and Mummy made them sit around the table before they ate their lunch. Every year, she got them to say what they were thankful for and what important lessons they had learned. After that, they had a delicious lunch and then spent the rest of the day relaxing.

"John, what are you thankful for?" Mummy asked.

"I'm thankful for all the kind things that people have done for me this year," John said. "It's inspired me to be kind as well and value friendship even more and show everyone around me how much I care about them".

Then, it was Sally's turn. "I'm thankful for all the teachers who helped me at school. They taught me my lessons, but also that it's important to speak to people and value support whenever you need it".

Finally, it was Joe's turn. "I'm thankful for the generosity of everyone I know. I want to show my gratitude even more next year because I've learned that even though people will give you gifts, the real magic of Christmas is about giving, not receiving".

They reflected on those thoughts while they are their wonderful Christmas lunch. Today, they were feeling nothing but joy because it was Christmas Day and they were spending it with the people they loved most. The children were growing up and they wanted to be able to celebrate the joys of Christmas without forgetting the important morals of the season.

Santa listened to the children say what they were thankful for, and he was overjoyed to know that they remembered that Christmas was about more than just gifts. It was the season of happiness, but only if everybody came together to make other people happy too.

He was standing on the roof of the house, ready to fly back to the North Pole. John, Sally and Joe were the last children on his list to deliver presents to, so he waited on the roof to let the reindeer rest before they had to go home.

As he climbed into his sleigh, Santa called out to the children in the house below him:

"Ho, ho, ho! Merry Christmas to you all! Remember everything that you have learned!"

John, Sally and Joe all rushed to the window after they heard the voice. They knew it had to be Santa.

Outside, the sleigh flew through the air, carrying Santa back to the North Pole where he would spend the year observing all the children in the world and preparing their presents.

The children waved up at him, knowing that Santa had given them the greatest gift of all: the joy of Christmas Day!

DISCLAIMER

This book contains opinions and ideas of the author and is meant
to teach the reader informative and helpful knowledge while
due care should be taken by the user in the application of the
information provided. The instructions and strategies are possibly
not right for every reader and there is no guarantee that they work
for everyone. Using this book and implementing the information/
recipes therein contained is explicitly your own responsibility
and risk. This work with all its contents, does not guarantee
correctness, completion, quality or correctness of the provided
information. Misinformation or misprints cannot be completely
eliminated.

Printed in Great Britain
by Amazon